This edition published by Parragon Books Ltd in 2014 and distributed by

Parragon Inc.
440 Park Avenue South, 13th Floor
New York, NY 10016
www.parragon.com

Written by Peter Bently
Edited by Laura Baker
Production by Charlene Vaughan

Illustrated by Emma Foster, Deborah Melmon and Henry St. Leger
Characters developed by Deborah Melmon
Designed by Alex Dimond and Creative Sweet

ISBN 978-1-4723-3241-7

Printed in China

Bunny Loves to Learn

PaRragon

Bath · New York · Singapore · Hong Kong · Cologne · Delhi
Melbourne · Amsterdam · Johannesburg · Shenzhen

One morning, Buster and his friends Sam, Max, and Francine arrived at school. "What's in those boxes, Mrs. Brooks?" asked Buster.

"Costumes!" said Mrs. Brooks. "Today you're going to dress up as people who lived a long time ago. I want you to learn all about these people, then make something from the time when they lived and tell us all about it in a dress-up show-and-tell!"

I love dressing up!

"I'm going to learn all about Vikings," said Buster. "This cloak is really cool!"

"I want to find out about knights," said Sam.
"They have amazing helmets!"

SEARCH: *knight*

Some knights decorated their helmets with colored feathers called plumes.

"Look at this dress,"
said Francine. "I think
I'll dress up as a princess!
I've always wanted to
learn more about them."

"I can't decide what to find out about," said Max.

"Why don't you dress up as an Egyptian ruler?" said Buster, taking a book from the shelf. "They were called pharaohs."

A ruler of Egypt was called a pharaoh.

Crown

Eye makeup

False beard

Jewelry

Kilt or skirt

But the pharaoh's crown was missing from the box.
"I don't want to be a ruler without a crown!" said Max.

Francine showed Max a website she was looking at.

"How about dressing up as a Roman boy?" she suggested.

"That outfit looks boring," said Max.

"Or a Roman soldier?" said Sam. "Look at that cool helmet!"

But the soldier costume in the box was much too big for Max.

Suddenly, Max pointed to a poster on the classroom wall.

"I want to learn about an Egyptian mummy!" he said. "Mummies are cool!"

"What about an Egyptian daddy?" joked Sam.

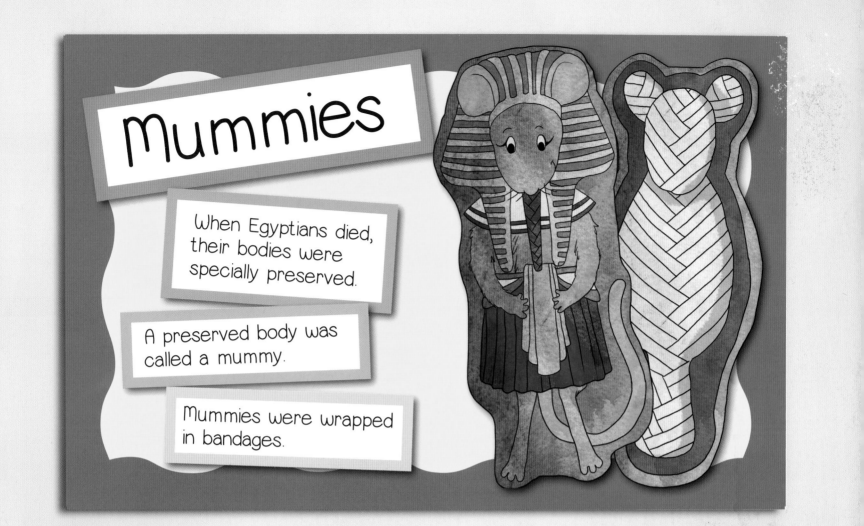

Mummies

When Egyptians died, their bodies were specially preserved.

A preserved body was called a mummy.

Mummies were wrapped in bandages.

"It's a *mummy*, not a mommy!" laughed Max. He rummaged in the costume box.

"Oh, no," he said. "There's no mummy costume."

While Max looked through the box, Sam said, "I have a knight's sword and a helmet. All I need is a shield. I'm going to make one!"

"Why does the helmet open and close?" asked Buster.

Sam looked in one of his books. "It closes to protect the knight when he is fighting in a battle," he said.

"But then, how could they tell which knight was which?" asked Francine.

"Good point," said Sam. "Let's see if it says in my book ..."

Helmets and Shields

Helmet

The visor protected the knight's face in battle. It had holes to see through.

Visor up

Visor down

Feather or plume

Each knight had a different shield.
This made it easy to recognize the knight when his visor was down.

Here it is!

Soon Buster, Sam, and Francine were busy making things.

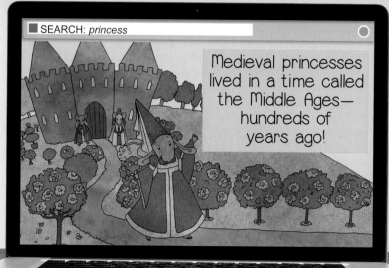

"I'm building a model of a Viking ship," said Buster.

"And I'm making a palace for a princess," said Francine.

But Max still didn't know what to make or learn about.

"I can't think of anything better than dressing as a mummy," he grumbled.

"What else do you know about Egyptians?" asked Buster.

"I know some of them built huge pyramids," said Max.

"Why don't you build one of those?" suggested Buster.

"Good idea!" said Max.

Max found some big pieces of cardboard and tried to make a pyramid. But somehow, it didn't look right.

"Oh, no," he said. "This is harder than I thought."

"We'll help you," said Buster. "We're almost done."

Buster and Sam helped Max find some books.

The base of a pyramid is a square.

An Egyptian pyramid has four sides. Each side is a triangle.

Francine showed him how to search for pyramids on the computer.

SEARCH: Egyptian pyramids

Egyptians used string to measure their pyramids carefully.

"Ah, now I see," said Max. "A pyramid has four sides, not three. And each side is exactly the same size. No wonder this one is so lopsided!"

Max finished his pyramid proudly, but then he sighed.
"I still don't know what to wear!" he said.

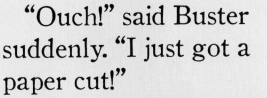

"Ouch!" said Buster suddenly. "I just got a paper cut!"

"It's just a little one," said Mrs. Brooks. "But you'd better go and see the school nurse for a bandage."

"OK," said Buster. "And I've just had an idea!" He whispered in Max's ear.

"Awesome!" laughed Max. "Please hurry up!"

When it was time for the class's show-and-tell, the friends took turns sharing what they had learned.

"I'm a knight," said Sam. "My shield protected me in battle. It was brightly painted so that my friends could recognize me when my helmet was shut!"

Then it was Francine's turn.
"I'm a princess," said Francine. "I lived
in a palace. I wore long dresses and tall
pointy hats. And I got to be involved in
the kingdom's politics!"

When he came back from the nurse, Buster showed the class his Viking ship. "I'm a Viking," he said. "I loved to sail in a longship. It had a dragon's head carved on the front to scare my enemies!"

"Thanks, Buster," said Mrs. Brooks. "Now it's Max's turn."

"Egyptians lived a very, very long time ago," said Max's voice. But he was nowhere to be seen. Where was he?

"They built amazing pyramids," the voice went on. "The pyramids were taller than ten houses on top of each other! Nobody lived in them, except for—

"MUMMIES! RAAAAH!"

And Max leapt out of the pyramid!

"So that's where you were hiding!" cried Francine.

"Where did you get that amazing mummy costume?" asked Sam. "I thought there wasn't one."

"I borrowed the bandages from the school nurse," said Max. "It was Buster's idea. Thanks for helping me, Buster!"

"Smart thinking, Buster! said Mrs. Brooks. "And all of you did a great job. Your costumes look amazing, and you've all learned some really interesting things. What a wonderful show-and-tell!"